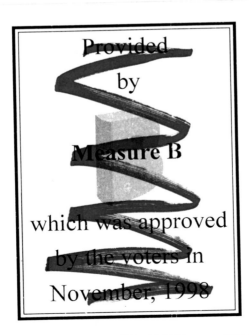

Provided

by

Measure B

which was approved

by the voters in

November, 1998

CAT AND DOG

by Else Holmelund Minarik

Pictures by Fritz Siebel

An I CAN READ Book®

HarperCollins*Publishers*

I CAN READ Books
by Else Holmelund Minarik
Pictures by Maurice Sendak

LITTLE BEAR
FATHER BEAR COMES HOME
LITTLE BEAR'S FRIEND
LITTLE BEAR'S VISIT
NO FIGHTING, NO BITING!

HarperCollins®, ®, and I Can Read Book®
are trademarks of HarperCollins Publishers Inc.

CAT AND DOG

CAT AND DOG

"Woof! Woof!

Off the bed,

Cat, Cat,

"Or I'll make

A catball out of you,

I will, I will."

"Meow, meow,

I'll get off,

I will, I will."

7

"Woof! Woof!

Off the chair,

Cat, Cat,

8

"Or I'll make

A catcoat out of you,

I will, I will."

9

"Meow, meow,

I'll get off,

I will, I will."

11

"Woof! Woof!

Off the table,

Cat, Cat,

"Or I'll make

A catpie out of you,

I will, I will."

13

"Meow, meow,

Come and get me,

Dog, Dog,

If you can,

If you can."

15

"Here! Here!

Off the table,

Silly Dog,

Silly Cat.

16

"Animals on the table!

My goodness!

The very idea."

"Meow—Meow—

Out of the water,

Dog, Dog.

You will make the house wet,

You will, you will."

"Woof! Woof!

Here I come.

Here I come."

"Meow—Meow—

Out of the garden,

Dog, Dog.

You will be tied up—

You will, you will."

"Woof! Woof!

Here I come.

I am coming."

24

"Meow—Meow—

Here are bones,

Dog, Dog.

Get them out.

Get them out."

"Woof! Woof!
Bones for me
—and for you.
Bones for us."

28

"Here! Here!

Silly Cat.

Silly Dog.

What is this?

30

"Are you so hungry?

Well, then,

I will feed you.

"Are you happy now?

Good."